Falling For The Warrens

Kit Kyndall

Published by Amourisa Press, 2020.

Kit Tunstall, writing as Kit Kyndall, reserves all rights to FALLING FOR THE WARRENS. Any resemblance to people or places is a coincidence. Please respect the copyright by not sharing this work. Permission of the author or publisher is required to copy any part of this work.

© Kit Kyndall, 2019

Cover image: Depositphoto

Cover design by Amourisa Designs

Join Kit's Mailing List[1] (www.kittunstall.com/newsletter) to receive notification of new releases and access bonus chapters for your favorite books. You get free books just for signing up! If you prefer to receive notifications for just one, or a few, of Kit's pen names, you'll have the option to select which lists to subscribe to at signup.

---

1. http://kittunstall.com/newsletter/

Blurb

Three tempting men, one bold choice, and things will never be the same.

HEATHER ROSS IS IN the Warren home to meet her boyfriend's family. Identical Daniel, so like her Michael, is pure temptation. Cliff, the elder Warren is a sexy silver fox. How is she supposed to resist temptation like this? What if her boyfriend doesn't want her to resist? What if he wants to share her with the most important men in his life?

Pure Escapes are steamy novellas that get right to the point. There's OTT alphas, crazy insta-love, heart-pounding desire, and improbable scenarios. They're pure escapist fantasies. Enjoy!

1

HEATHER ROSS'S NERVES clenched her stomach into a tight ball as she stepped into the elegant house with her boyfriend, Michael Warren. He held onto her hand, and she used it to steady herself as she prepared to meet Michael's family. He had a brother and a father, and though she and Michael had been dating five months, she hadn't met the others yet.

Now that they were done with school, having graduated their bachelor's degrees a couple of days ago, Michael had invited her to spend the summer with him at the Warren home, where he still officially lived. It was a big step forward, and she was ready. She was also nervous about making a good impression on his family.

"Relax. They're going to love you." There was a strange gleam in his eyes for a moment. "Daniel's really going to love you."

She frowned at that, not certain what meant, but before she could ask, they'd passed through the foyer and into the living room. Two identical dark heads sat in wingback chairs, both staring at the television, where some sports game was playing. She could identify it as soccer but didn't know anything beyond that.

"We're home," said Michael.

With a flurry of activity, the two men who'd been sitting stood up and turned to face them. Heather's knees immediately went weak, but not from nerves. "You never told me Daniel was your identical twin." There was a note of accusation in her voice, and color swept into her cheeks when she met Daniel's eyes. They were appraising, and she immediately saw a hint of attraction there. Had that been what Michael meant earlier? That he and his brother shared similar taste in women, so Daniel was sure to like her?

The thought made her toes curl in her sandals. It sparked heat lower in her belly, and she was suddenly damp at the idea of having Michael and Daniel touching her. The moisture increased when she looked away from Daniel and got her first glimpse of Michael's father.

Cliff Warren must've been the original mold from which the twins were cast, and he favored them greatly. He was a harder, firmer, older version of them. They all had deep black hair and smoldering blue eyes a shade lighter than Navy. She was suddenly so turned on she wanted to turn throw herself into Michael's arms and mount him right there.

Somehow, she managed to regain her composure and held out her hand when Cliff extended his to shake. Just the touch of his hand against hers set her skin tingling and heat sweeping all the way up her arm that spread throughout her body. There was a similar effect when she touched Daniel's hand a moment later. She was a sodden mess, and her nipples were poking through her sundress so hard that she doubted anybody could miss them.

Especially Daniel, whose gaze was boldly on them, clearly admiring her pert breasts. His gaze lifted to meet her eyes, and he winked at her.

"Why don't you get our guest settled into her room, and we'll order Thai food?" said Cliff.

"We probably won't be hungry for an hour so. We had lunch before we left the University," said Michael.

Cliff nodded. "In that case, we'll delay ordering for a bit." His gaze focused on Heather, and he smiled. It was a warm expression, and it sent heat spiraling through her. "Feel free to make yourself at home here, Heather, and use anything you might want for your pleasure."

The words sounded positively sinful, but that could just be her own perception, and the way she immediately imagined how she might get pleasure from all three of the men surrounding her. What was wrong with her? She shook her head, trying to clear her thoughts, as Michael led her farther down the hall to a staircase.

They climbed together, and she admired the house. Far more than functional, it was obvious the Warren family had money. Having grown up mostly without it, she was a little awed and intimidated, and she was glad she and Michael had been dating for a while before she discovered his affluent background, not wanting him to think she was after his money.

"You have this room," said Michael as he opened a set of double doors and stepped inside, waving his hand for her to follow.

She stepped into the room and admired the blonde wood under her feet. It was so pale it was almost white, and the walls were a similar shade. The furniture was delicate and white as well, with lavender accents. "It's lovely. It has to be three times the size of my dorm room." Not that she'd spent much time in her dorm room for the last five months. She'd pretty much been living at Michael's apartment, which had been a sparse student unit, giving no hints to his true financial background.

"I figured you might want your own room, but you're always welcome to share my bed." As he said that, Michael closed the doors and came to stand behind her, cupping her biceps with his hands as the heat of his cock pressed against the curve of her ass. "Or I could share your bed."

Decorum dictated she absolutely shouldn't be hopping into bed with her boyfriend the moment they arrived at his dad's house. They should be socializing and getting better acquainted, but after the jolt she'd gotten from meeting his father and brother, she was in no shape to deny what her body wanted.

She didn't resist at all when Michael reached around and started unbuttoning the buttons on her dress. It fell to her feet a moment later, and the pink bra quickly followed. When she was in her matching panties, she turned to face him, helping him strip off his T-shirt before attacking his shorts with eager hands.

When they both stood in just their underwear, she cupped his ass through the cloth, enjoying the feel of his hard length pressing into her belly. He was a foot taller than her, with a solid frame, and he always made her feel protected and dainty.

He picked her up, and she wrapped her thighs around his waist. His mouth claimed hers in a hot, hungry kiss as he carried her to the bed and laid her down. Michael's mouth drifted down her chin to her to neck, where he sucked the bend, knowing how much it drove her wild. She writhed and twisted on the bed as his mouth did its magic while his fingers drifted lower, pushing aside her panties so he could stroke her bare slit.

He moaned in pleasure. "I love when you've just waxed."

She muttered something, which was a passable agreement. She knew how much he loved it, and that's why she kept doing it. It certainly wasn't because it was a fun experience, but having her mound completely bare made her so much more sensitive, so it was for both of them.

He stripped off her panties and tossed them aside before doing the same with his briefs. Then he knelt between her thighs. "Should I eat this pussy?"

She nodded her head and moaned as his tongue slipped down her abdomen to her slit. He paused there for a moment before tracing her outer lips with the lightest touch. "Michael, please." She was so desperate to feel him inside her, first his tongue and then his long, thick cock. "I need you."

"You're very wet," he said, and there was a strange inflection to his tone she couldn't decipher.

"I want you."

"I know you do." He chuckled. "Still, you're even wetter than usual. I wonder why?" He looked up at her.

She squirmed under the intensity of his gaze, her mind flashing to her instant attraction to both his brother and his father. Had he noticed? Was he calling her on it? Examining his expression, he didn't seem upset. He seemed hornier than usual too. Maybe he was excited by the idea of her being attracted to his brother?

Likely, he hadn't realized she'd had a similar response his father. She closed her eyes as forbidden images of both the twins touching her came to her, and she writhed again, lifting her hips in desperation.

2

MICHAEL FINALLY ACQUIESCED, pressing his mouth against her wet heat. His tongue slipped inside her, tracing around her clit previous to sweeping up and down her slit. He probed her opening before sliding back to her clit again with the broadside of his tongue. Then he used just the tip to trace her anatomy once more.

She cupped his head, holding him against her in one spot, since he kept trying to move away with maddening frequency. She didn't want him teasing her. She just wanted to come. She clutched him, directing his tongue to her clit, and rode his face as he sucked and licked her. When he inhaled before exhaling against her clit, it sent her over the edge, and she cried out her pleasure.

He sat up, wiping her arousal from his face before coming down again to kiss her. His tongue entered her mouth, offering her a taste of her own pleasure, and she licked his tongue before wrapping her arms around him to pull him closer.

"I love to watch you come. You're so amazing. So fucking beautiful, but never more beautiful than when you're getting off from something I've done." Michael lifted his head to say those words, and then he surprised her by leaning back the other direction, taking her with him.

Soon, she was straddling his stomach. "Ride me, Heather. Let me see that beautiful hair of yours in my face. Fuck me."

She was shaking in her eagerness, and it barely registered that she'd already orgasmed once. She was desperate and aching for him again, so she leaned back and rested her folds over the top of his hard cock. She rubbed a little bit, making him groan and release a surge of pre-cum. As wet as she was, she had no trouble sliding straight down his shaft, taking him fully inside her. They both grunted at the sense of completion as she sat on him for a moment before she started arching up and down.

Michael kept his hands on her hips, steadying her, but she set the pace. Their coupling was hard and frantic, and while she rode him, she bent forward so her hair could fall on his face. Then she bent a little lower, though it stretched her back, and kissed him deeply.

She looked up at the door when she thought she heard a creak. Heather gasped to see a pair of blue eyes staring through a crack between the opened doors, which Michael had closed. Daniel winked at her, making no move to leave. He was clearly planning to enjoy the show.

She should've been outraged and appalled. She should've screamed at him to leave them alone and should've marched over to close the door and lock it this time. She didn't do any of that. Instead, she met Daniel's gaze and licked her lips as she rode Michael hard and fast, needing the friction of his cock against her g-spot.

As she stared at Daniel while fucking Michael, Daniel open the door wider still. He was giving her his own show. He had opened his shorts, and he grasped his long cock in his hand. From the distance separating them, he seemed to be identical to Michael in that regard as well. He was long and thick, and her mouth watered for a taste of him.

He was stroking his cock in an almost frantic fashion, and it was the first sight of his seed spreading outward onto his hand that triggered her orgasm. She clamped hard around Michael, clinging to his shoulders, but not looking away from Daniel as he finished coming, nodded at her, and closed the door softly.

Her pleasure overwhelmed her, and as Michael came inside her, she collapsed against him, riding the waves of bliss. It was only after, when he turned them on their sides, that she realized what she'd done.

She'd eye-fucked Daniel while Michael was inside her. What kind of message had that sent? Daniel was likely expecting her to follow through on an unspoken promise now. She wasn't the type to cheat, and she was in love with Michael, so how could she have responded that way to Daniel? She couldn't understand it, and she was filled with guilt.

Michael didn't seem to realize. He pressed a kiss to her forehead. "I know you want to shower, so I'll swing by my room to drop off my things, and then I'll be downstairs. Come down when you're ready." He kissed her again before getting off the bed.

She just nodded at him, watching him go. She laid there for a long moment, feeling his release inside her while she tortured herself with guilt at what she'd done. It was a form of cheating, wasn't it? Suddenly, she couldn't stand that Michael didn't know. She hated to confess her sin, but she didn't feel like she could hide it from him. She also needed Michael to keep her strong, because Daniel presented too much temptation.

Not to mention Cliff, whispered a seductive voice in the back of her mind. She quickly squashed that as she got out of bed. She fumbled with her sundress and slipped it on, certain she'd missed a couple of buttons, but not too concerned as she slipped from her room to find Michael's.

Her stomach clenched with anxiety as she pictured telling him what had happened. She didn't want to come between the brothers, and it occurred to her Michael might be angry with Daniel. Maybe she shouldn't say anything after all? She paused outside his doorway, second-guessing the wisdom of confessing what had happened, which allowed her a moment to realize Michael wasn't alone.

"She's fucking hot, Michael. I want to be balls' deep inside her."

Michael chuckled. "I'm not surprised. We've always had similar taste. Heather's different though. She's special to me, and I don't think she's the type who'd want to be shared. You'll just have to settle for fantasizing and your own hand."

Daniel groaned. "That's really unfair. How can you bring her here, parade her in front of me, and then say she's off-limits?"

"I didn't say she was off-limits."

Heather's eyes widened at the words, and she put a hand over her mouth to stifle a gasp of shock.

"That would be Heather's decision, not mine," said Michael, sounding remarkably unconcerned about the idea of his brother lusting after his girlfriend. "I knew you'd want her, but I don't think she'll do that." Did Michael sound regretful? His tone certainly suggested he wasn't happy about his perceived assumption she wouldn't be open to letting his brother touch her.

Heather pressed a hand to her galloping heart as she leaned against the wall. Her pussy throbbed with renewed arousal while she listened to them talk about her. She bit her tongue to keep in a moan when Daniel said, "I can't help picturing bending her over to slide into that hot pussy while you feel her mouth wrapped around your cock. Are you sure she's not down for that?"

Heather held her breath as she waited to see what Michael would say. She wasn't even certain what she would say if either one of them asked her. Before the opportunity presented itself, she would've assumed she'd immediately reject the idea, but now here it was. Did she really want to be shared by Michael and Daniel?

3

AN ACHING THROB BETWEEN her thighs confirmed she did.

"Like I said, it's up to Heather. You know I don't mind sharing, but I can't speak for her."

Having heard enough, and abandoning her plan to confess, she rushed back to the guestroom and closed the door, locking it behind her. She leaned her forehead against the wood, gasping for breath as images of being shared by the twins flooded through her.

She dug her fingers into her pussy, almost punishing it for its need as she rubbed herself hard with two fingers. She was wet from their words and made slipperier by the remaining cum Michael had left inside her. Imagining having Michael and Daniel both cum inside her was enough to send her over the edge again, and she bit her lip as she moaned softly. Her knees weakened, and she leaned heavily against the door for a moment as she struggled to regain her composure.

When she could stand once more, she rushed to the shower and washed off. She could clean off the cum, but she couldn't wash away her thoughts. Filthy, illicit thoughts of having two men. If Daniel and Michael were okay with it, it wouldn't be wrong, would it? Traditional social mores suggested she should be horrified at the idea, but she couldn't pretend like it didn't excite her.

She hadn't yet made up her mind, and she wasn't even confident they would really ask her to fuck both of them at the same time, but she was still thinking about it as she dried off. Her pussy was supersensitive from her recent activities, and the towel managed to turn her on all over again.

She walked out of the bathroom and went to the bed, lying down with her legs splayed as she started touching herself another time. Had she suddenly turned into a nympho? This was insane. She'd already had three orgasms, and here she was, chasing a fourth.

She closed her eyes, imagining two mouths at her breasts while a thick cock slid between her thighs. In her fantasy, her eyes were closed as well. She arched against her hand, imagining it was a thick cock instead. She opened her eyes in the fantasy and discovered Michael and Daniel were the ones feasting on her breasts, and Cliff was the one fucking her. She came with a cry she couldn't hold in, her entire body shaking from it, and leaving her a wet mess.

Maybe she should go home. She didn't have a real home to go to, since her mother was with her newest boyfriend, and Heather had never even met him. She could go visit friends, though she'd drifted somewhat from her best friend when she started dating Michael, and she'd been unable to tear herself away from him when it wasn't absolutely necessary, like for class. They still socialized sometimes with their friends, but things had changed.

She didn't want to go anywhere. She wanted to be with Michael, but she was afraid the intensity of what she was feeling would overwhelm common sense, and she might do something she'd regret.

There was a knock on her door suddenly, and she jumped. Her fingers were still buried in her pussy, and she pulled them out with a guilty feeling as she got to her feet and grabbed the robe in her suitcase. She shrugged it on, tying the belt with clumsy fingers before she rushed to the door. She opened it after unlocking it, and her stomach dipped in a slow, sinuous way when she opened it to find Cliff standing on the other side.

He was leaning against the doorframe, and he just looked so casually confident he made her mouth water. He had obvious lines around his eyes and in his forehead that the twins didn't have, but it didn't make him any less attractive. It just added a new layer of appeal, and once again, her thighs clenched as her pussy throbbed.

If she couldn't get this under control, she'd spend all day either fucking or masturbating. That wasn't exactly an unappealing idea, and it didn't do anything to help her stop thinking about the moment she'd imagined Cliff's cock in her pussy. Her face heated at the memory.

He frowned, looking concerned. "I came to see what you wanted me to order you from the Thai restaurant, but you don't look well. Are you okay?"

She fanned her face as her blush increased. "I'm fine. I'm just..." She trailed off as his nostrils flared. Realizing she was fanning herself with the hand she'd used to masturbate, she quickly dropped it to her side. Had he smelled it? Did he know what she'd been doing?

Briefly meeting his gaze, she was certain he did. His eyes had darkened, and he looked aroused. There was a faint hint of color to his cheekbones, and she moaned softly when she realized he found her as attractive as she found him.

"What's wrong, Heather?" His voice deepened slightly, taking on a husky note.

She should have just sent him away with a lame excuse, but before she could think better of it, she said, "I overheard a conversation between Daniel and Michael." Could her face get any hotter? She must be as red as a fire engine by now.

He arched a brow, and then sudden comprehension appeared in his eyes. "Ah."

She tilted her head slightly. "What does that mean?"

His gaze moved down her body for a moment before returning to her eyes. "I can infer what they might have been discussing. Was Daniel...admiring you?"

She nodded, unable to look away from his compelling gaze. She licked her lips, and he moaned softly. "He said he liked me. Well, he didn't put it quite like that."

Cliff's mouth turned up in a slight smile. "I can imagine what colorful language he used. He said he wanted to fuck you?"

When he said that word, it made her tremble, and she clenched her thighs tighter together. "He wants to be in my pussy while Michael is in my mouth." She blanched, realizing what she'd just said to her boyfriend's father. The way she said it was more like an invitation than information she was sharing.

He swallowed audibly for a moment, his gaze dipping down to her breasts. He continued staring there for a moment, and she looked down.

No wonder he was studying her breasts. She hadn't fully dried off, and the white silk robe did nothing to hide her dusky pink areolas or her tight nipples. When she imagined his mouth covering them through the silk robe, they hardened even further.

His gaze returned to hers. "They've shared girls in the past."

Her mouth dropped open. "You were okay with that?"

He shrugged a shoulder. "I figured it was between them and the girl, to be honest. They're twins. They're a lot alike, and they have very similar tastes. I'm not surprised Daniel wants you as much as Michael does. They've always gone for petite blondes with big blue eyes. You're just their type. You're a sexy young woman."

It should've been impossible, but her flush deepened. "Th...thank you."

He inclined his head. "It's certainly something to think about, isn't it?"

Her brain felt a little behind. "What?"

"Having more than one lover at the same time. Multiple hands and mouths to please you, hard, thick cocks for your pleasure—just some things to think about."

She nodded, need consuming her as she was unable to think about anything else. "I..."

With a grin, he took her hand, the very one she'd been using to stroke her pussy, and lifted it to his mouth. She expected to feel his tongue or his lips, but instead, he just inhaled deeply. His pupils widened, and he exhaled harshly a moment later. "What do you want from the Thai place?"

She couldn't think about such things now, so she picked the first thing she could recall. "Pad Thai."

He nodded. "One of my favorites." His tongue darted out of his mouth, lightly running across her fingers to taste her essence. "Delicious." He definitely wasn't talking about pad Thai.

When he let go of her hand, she drew it back to her side and stared at him helplessly as he nodded at her. "It usually takes about a half-hour for them to deliver, so you have time to see to your needs before then."

He spoke that in a very sensual way, winking at her, before standing up and walking down the hall. He didn't look back, but she watched him until she could no longer see him. Then she closed the door and leaned against it, hand once more frantically seeking out her swollen, hot flesh to coax forth another orgasm. This time, her thoughts were on all three of them, and she didn't have any guilt at the idea.

4

HEATHER SOMEHOW COMPOSED herself enough to look like she hadn't just spent the last hour having orgasms and forbidden fantasies. She put on a fresh sundress, but she didn't bother with a bra. What was the point of panties as well? The soft, silky fabric of the dress caressed her bare ass with each step, making her feel hot and flustered all over again.

She found the dining room easily enough, since the house wasn't quite that large, and there was a Styrofoam container waiting for her beside an empty plate. Michael and Daniel already had their food arranged on their plates, and Cliff was in the process of doing so with his.

She wasn't able to meet any of their gazes completely, but her greeting sounded reasonably normal as she took a seat. She started dishing out her food, focusing all her attention on it so she didn't look up and make a fool of herself by meeting the wrong knowing gaze.

"Tell us about yourself," said Cliff.

She did look up then, briefly meeting his gaze and flushing before staring deliberately over his shoulder instead. "I don't think there's really much to tell. I just graduated with a degree in communications. Until a few years ago, I had your typical suburban life. My parents were happy and in love, and they loved me. When my dad died unexpectedly, my mom kind of went off the rails."

"How do you mean?" asked Daniel, his gaze boring into hers. He seemed to want to know everything about her. Was that a little intense for just sexual attraction? It should be, but it didn't feel excessive or intrusive.

She cleared her throat. "She started drinking dating a lot. She sold our house and moved in with one guy after another. I was away at college shortly after Dad's passing, but it's definitely driven a wedge between us. I know she's lonely and looking to replace what she had with my dad, but she's acting a bit like a desperate tramp."

Talk about words hitting close to home. Guilt pierced her again when she thought about the fact she was attracted to all three of the men around the table. She didn't want to be like her mother, though she doubted her mom was entertaining ideas of taking three lovers, especially from the same family. Was she even worse than her mom?

"There's nothing wrong with having sex if it makes you feel good," said Cliff. "I hope she's not hurting herself in the long run by falling for guys that aren't going to be there for her, but I don't see anything shameful about her behavior."

It was almost like he'd guessed Heather's thoughts, and his words were directed to soothe her rather than about her mom. Was she just reading too much into it? She didn't know, which left her confused and flustered. She just nodded as she looked down, going through the mechanics of taking a bite of the pad Thai. It was spicy and delicious, but she could barely focus on anything besides them and the conflict she felt.

"The only thing Cheryl's done wrong is exclude you from her new life," said Michael with a grimace. He knew the whole story, and she knew he disapproved of her mother no longer making her a priority.

She took his hand, smiling at him. "Thank you."

He leaned over and pressed a kiss to her forehead. "You know how I feel about it, but I agree with my dad. There's no harm in having sex with whomever you want just for pleasure."

Was she imagining a double meaning in his words, or a subtle subtext he planned to infer? Darting her gaze between him and Daniel, as they looked at each other with similar expressions, she didn't think she was. Could she really let them share her? She had no doubt it would be amazing and intense, but would it damage her relationship with Michael afterward? She loved him and respected him, but what if he changed how he looked at her, or she changed how she looked at him? What if she fell in love with Daniel as well as Michael?

Before she could think better of it, she blurted out, "When you've shared girls, did you both fall in love with them?"

Daniel and Michael froze, sharing twin expressions of shock.

Heather glanced at Cliff, finding him mildly amused. She looked away again, focusing on Michael, since she was most comfortable with him. "I came to talk to you after you left my room, and I overheard your conversation with Daniel. Your dad told me you guys have shared girls before, but how does that work? Is it strictly physical, or are emotions involved too?"

"It's been both ways," said Michael.

Daniel picked up from there. "We've had girlfriends we shared."

She looked at him, seeing the naked desire in his expression. "Girlfriends, as in relationships?"

Daniel nodded. "The longest we dated the same girl was about eight months. We might've gone longer, but we were all going to separate colleges, and Brooke was heading across the country. None of us wanted a long-distance relationship."

She frowned. "And you were both in love with her?"

Daniel nodded, and Michael murmured his agreement. "And she was in love with both of you?"

"She said she was," said Michael. "I suppose she could've been lying, but it didn't feel like it."

"What about the other kind of sharing?"

"Those have mostly been one-night stands or friends-with-benefits situations," said Daniel casually.

Michael nodded. "A lot of girls have fantasies of being shared by twins, so there's a never-ending supply of pussy if we want it. The thing is, we both like to have a bigger connection than just sex. We often have very similar tastes and feel the same way about things." He said that with a hint of meaning as he leaned forward to kiss her lips. "We're totally secure with sharing all our things."

She frowned. "A girlfriend isn't a thing."

Michael nodded. "I didn't mean it like that. I just meant that we don't have jealousy whether we're sharing a girl or sharing a BMW."

She was briefly sidetracked. "You have a BMW?"

"It was their eighteenth birthday present," said Cliff, finally contributing to the conversation. His voice was husky, and he was clearly enjoying what was playing out before him.

"Only one," she teased for a moment, grinning at Cliff, who grinned in return.

"They were only eighteen. And they'd been sharing all kinds of things for years."

She wrinkled her brow. "When did you two start sharing girls?"

"We were fifteen," said Daniel. "She was an older girl at school, and it was her idea, but we didn't mind."

She rubbed her forehead. "And it's just the girls you share? You guys aren't...?" She trailed off with a grimace of disgust.

Michael's nose curled. "If you're asking if we share each other, fuck no. It's all about you...her," he corrected, but not in time.

She suspected it had been a Freudian slip, or perhaps a deliberate phrasing to make her think about the two of them using her body. It wouldn't be using though, would it? She'd be getting an amazing amount of pleasure she could barely even imagine.

She cleared her throat and met Cliff's gaze. He gave her an encouraging nod, so she turned back to Michael and then darted her gaze to Daniel, who sat across the table. "And you want to share me?"

"More than fucking anything," said Daniel with a groan.

She nodded at him, but her gaze remained on Michael. "If you love me, is it going to weird you out or make you jealous?"

"No, not at all." He sounded confident. "And of course, I love you. No *if* about it."

She bit her lip. "What would happen if I fell in love with Daniel and you?"

"It wouldn't bother me. In fact, it's a distinct possibility since Daniel and I are a lot alike. I'm not bothered by you loving other men as long as you still love me." His gaze moved pointedly to Cliff for a long second before returning to her. Was he sending the message that it was okay for her to want his father too? He must have picked up on the vibe between them.

She turned her attention to Cliff. "And do you share with your sons?"

Cliff shook his head. "They've never dated anyone I wanted before."

Her stomach dipped in disappointment, and she nodded as she started to look away.

"Until now," added Cliff in a raspy voice.

5

HER GAZE DARTED BACK to his, and she saw the banked desire there. She looked at Michael, uncertain what his reaction might be to the acknowledgment from his father that he found his girlfriend attractive. Michael looked serene.

He smiled at her. "We're a very close family. Some might say it'd be ideal to find a woman who pleases us all so we can be together."

She trembled at the thought, but she didn't move away when Daniel stood up to come around the table. He knelt beside her after moving the chair on her other side, putting a hand on her thigh. She trembled at the touch, especially when Michael put his hand on her other thigh in the same spot, and they squeezed in tandem.

She closed her eyes when Daniel leaned closer, sweeping his lips against her cheek. She turned her head to meet his mouth, shaking from the intensity of her reaction when his lips brushed gently against hers. He didn't try to rush anything. It was an exploratory kiss, one that invited her to deepen it, but he didn't take the initiative to do so.

With gasping breaths, she lifted an arm and put it around Daniel's shoulders, pulling him a little closer as she shyly dipped her tongue into his mouth. He let her set the pace, but she quickly increased. She was consumed with need, and Michael's hand having drifted from her thigh to her breast was spurring that.

Fingers undid her buttons, though she wasn't certain to which brother the hand belonged. A second later, both of her breasts were being touched, and she discovered a slight difference. Daniel had calluses on his fingertips that Michael lacked. It provided a new texture and sensation, and she writhed in the chair as Daniel took over the kiss, becoming more commanding and forceful as he cupped her chin and tipped her head back so his mouth covered hers, and his tongue could surge inside.

Their mouths mated with wild abandon as her tongue stroked his. Michael knew just the right way to pinch and roll her nipple, and Daniel soon picked up the pattern. It was amazing and intense, and for what seemed like the millionth time that day, she was suddenly filled with desire and wanted them inside her.

Daniel pulled back. "You taste delicious. No wonder Michael can't get enough of you." As he spoke, his thumb continued to drift around her nipple. "Is it all right if I see more of you?"

With a whimper, she nodded. She expected them to take her from the dining room, but instead, Daniel stood up and moved their plates out of the way before he and Michael lifted her onto the table. Michael finished unbuttoning her sundress so that it was opened, baring her body. She turned her head to meet Cliff's gaze, wondering why he hadn't joined them.

He was leaning back, watching everything, and it was obvious from the way his hand was moving that he was stroking his cock under the table. She licked her lips and tried issuing an invitation with her eyes, but he remained where he was. She frowned in confusion, thinking she might've misinterpreted what he wanted from her.

Before she could dwell on it, Daniel had moved again, this time between her thighs. Michael moved to the other side of the table, by her head, leaning forward to kiss her upside down, his mouth claiming hers with fierce possession. He didn't mind sharing, or so he claimed, but he clearly wanted to leave his mark on her as well. She was completely fine with that, and she resisted when his mouth tried to move away from hers, twining her hand in his hair to hold him against her for another moment.

He pushed through her resistance, his mouth moving down, and she surrendered after a moment when he cupped both of her breasts in his hands, extending his tongue so he could lick her nipples as he moved his head back and forth quickly.

Daniel hadn't been idle. He had her feet propped on chairs now, and her ass was at the edge of the table. He knelt, kissing her pussy in almost the same way he had her lips. It was gentle and exploratory to start with, his tongue barely tasting her. When he suddenly dipped inside, darting into her opening with a fierce thrust of his appendage, she whimpered and arched her back.

The mouth on her pussy moved back. "She tastes like ambrosia," said Daniel, clearly addressing the remark to Michael.

"Her breasts her sweet and luscious too. You have to taste them sometime, Daniel."

It was her body they were talking about, and their comments were naughty, but it only further revved her desire for them. She arched her hips once more, inviting Daniel deeper inside. His tongue squirmed in her sheath for a bit before drifting up slowly, the side of his tongue eliciting all sorts of sensations.

When his mouth fastened around her clit, it throbbed in response, and she arched once more, her ass practically off the table now. Daniel's hands moved to support her buttocks as he held her up so he could feast on her voraciously. His mouth increased its pace, and her pussy responded by shuddering and twitching. It was good, but she wanted more.

With Michael still sucking on her nipples and alternating between gentle nips and hard bites, she was a writhing mass of sensation. She still felt like there was a missing element, and she turned to look at Cliff. He leaned farther back now, and she could see the top of his cock above the table line, his hand working it furiously. If she'd touched him like that, she would've been afraid of hurting him, but clearly his steely erection could take the punishment. He was breathing heavily, and she wondered why he didn't join them.

She was distracted from that thought when Daniel stopped licking her, leaving her on the edge of coming. She made a sound of protest, and Daniel leaned over so he could look into her eyes, without Michael blocking his view. "Is it all right if I fuck you? Can I put my cock in your sweet, hot pussy?"

She hovered on the edge of acquiescence, knowing giving her permission was fundamentally changing things in ways she might not even realize yet. This was her last chance to do what would be considered the right thing and call this off. The problem was, she had no desire to do that. She wanted to feel Daniel inside her, so she nodded. "Please. I want to feel every inch of you."

"That's good. Is it okay if I fuck you raw? I saw you take Michael without a condom, so is it okay if I do that? I want to be inside you and feel everything, and I promise you I'm clean. You're protected?"

She nodded. "I'm on the pill, and I'm clean. You can fuck me raw." Saying those words brought a flush to her cheeks, reminding her she was normally a lot more inhibited about such things. Michael had woken a passionate animal inside her, but in her everyday life, she was usually much more circumspect when it came to sex. She'd certainly never uttered the phrase fucked raw before. She'd never have guessed how freeing it was, or how it made her feel like an experienced seductress.

"And since Michael's being such a good brother and sharing this sweet little pussy with me, will you suck his cock? Is that all right with you?"

Heather nodded, opening her mouth. Michael's lips moved away from her breasts, to her regret, and they shifted her once again, this time so her head was hanging slightly over the table. Daniel kept his hands under her ass, tilting her pelvis at an incline, and Michael's cock rubbed against her lips.

She parted them to accept his erection, pre-cum coating her tongue with salty anticipation. She opened her mouth as wide as she could so he could slide deeply inside her. Michael knew just when to stop, reaching the back of her throat and letting her adjust before he started stroking himself into her mouth.

She snugged her cheeks around him, licking the underside of his cock for a moment as fluid wept continuously onto her tongue. When she started sucking, Michael moaned as he arched his hips against her.

"All settled there, sweetheart?" asked Daniel.

With her mouth full of cock, she couldn't answer, so she lifted her hand to form an "okay" sign with her fingers. She gasped around Michael's cock when Daniel placed the head of his erection against her opening. He surged inside her with one deep, hard thrust, and she moaned at the sensation of having two cocks inside her.

She wondered if Cliff was enjoying the show, but she couldn't really turn her head to find out. As though her thoughts had summoned him, he came to stand nearby. From the corner of her eye, she saw his hand flying over his cock, and then it twitched. A second later, his cum splashed across her chest, and she shivered at the sensation. It was so good, but nothing compared to when he lifted a hand and started rubbing his cum all over her breast, focusing particularly on the nipple.

She lost control of everything at that point, twisting and bucking against Daniel while trying to remember to suck Michael. Cliff's hand on her breast was the final thing she needed, and she came around Daniel's cock with a cry muffled by Michael's shaft in her mouth.

Daniel's fingers dug into her buttocks almost painfully as he surged into her, bucking arrhythmically in his urgent need. Seconds later, he twitched and spasmed, shooting his load deep inside. The thought of his cum and Michael's mingling somewhere in her body spurred another orgasm, and she clamped tightly around him again as Michael spilled his seed down her throat.

She lost awareness after that, surrendering to the ecstasy that had overwhelmed her, and allowing the men to take care of her. She had no memory of getting from the dining room to the guestroom, though she was vaguely aware of a wet washcloth between her thighs and moving over her body. There were two identical kisses on her cheeks, but she was too exhausted to respond. Sleep slipped over her, and she succumbed to it willingly.

6

IT MUST'VE BEEN ONLY a little after dawn when she woke, because weak light was just starting to come through the curtains. Her body ached, but in a pleasant way, and she stretched as she remembered how she'd ended up in the bed.

She waited for guilt to overtake her, but it didn't come. Instead, she just felt deeply satisfied and happy that she had done something so out of character. The best part was, it didn't feel like it had been a one-time thing. She was certain Daniel wouldn't be eager to give her up now that he'd had her, and she felt the same way. She wanted Michael and Daniel both. She wasn't in love with Daniel the way she was with Michael yet, but she could see it happening easily.

She also wanted Cliff. An ache went through her when she recalled him holding back. Why? Maybe he needed to hear her explicitly invite him to join them? She wasn't sure, and she was afraid his limited participation in the dining room might be all he would give her, since she was with his son. Or was that sons now? She felt like she belonged with Daniel too.

It wouldn't be without precedent to feel so strongly so quickly. After all, she'd met Michael on a Monday in a shared class. He'd invited her out for coffee afterward. That Wednesday, they had a romantic dinner together, and she'd become his lover by Friday. She was virtually living with him a week later, and she'd first told him she loved him roughly two weeks after they met, once he'd said it first. She hadn't said it because it was expected either. She'd genuinely meant it and had in fact been holding back the words for days, not wanting to spook him.

It wasn't like Heather to rush in. Her earlier relationships had gone at much slower paces, but the ironic thing was, she hadn't felt like she'd known either one of her two previous boyfriends after months of dating with the same level of intimacy that she knew Michael by the end of one week.

It seemed logical that it could be the same with Daniel. And Cliff? He was a bit of an enigma, so she wasn't sure. She wanted to find out though.

There was a knock at her door, and she stiffened. She rolled out of bed and grabbed her robe, slinging it on carelessly, though it seemed hardly worth the bother now that all three of the Warren men had seen her naked. She padded to the door and opened it, surprised to see Cliff standing on the other side. She leaned against the door for support as her knees went weak at the sight of him.

He was wearing a black silk robe, and it was open almost all the way down. She could see the line of hair on his flat stomach that led to his cock if she followed it visually all the way down. Instead, she admired his toned abs, impressed by his body. He had to be in his early forties, but he looked as lean and toned as his sons. "Yes?"

"Will you come with me?"

She didn't hesitate. She stepped away from the door and followed him through it. He took her hand as they walked down the hall, and even that light contact was enough to send her body into overdrive. She started getting wet between the legs just holding his hand.

He led her down the hallway to the room at the end, behind another set of double doors, and he opened them to welcome her inside. His room was three times the size of hers, with black and silver as the predominant color scheme. Crisp splashes of red alleviated the monotone in a pleasing fashion, but she had little time to evaluate the decor.

Still holding her hand, he tugged her lightly through his bedroom and into the bathroom.

She stumbled to a stop, awed by the sight before her. There was a huge sunken tub, easily the size of a small swimming pool. Cliff had taken time to line the edge with candles and rose petals, and the water was perfumed with rose as well. It was an intoxicating scent, and she relaxed against him when he put his hands on her shoulders. She tipped her head back against his shoulder for a moment. "I was afraid you didn't want me."

"That's certainly not the case." As he spoke, Cliff grinded his pelvis against her ass, giving her proof of how much he wanted her. If possible, he was even longer and thicker than his sons. That was a little daunting, but she looked forward to the challenge.

"So why didn't you join us earlier?"

"I wanted our first time to be alone, and besides, you weren't ready."

She could've protested that, knowing she had been ready, but he stepped back and slipped off her robe. By the time he'd taken off his and took her hand to lead her into the hot water, she'd forgotten about wanting to ask for further clarification.

Cliff settled on a bench that was built into the tub, pulling her down on him to straddle his lap. He looked up at her. "I want to kiss you so badly."

She lowered her head, wanting the same thing. His lips were firm and confident, having no trouble demanding a response from her. She wouldn't have withheld it anyway, but she doubted she could've if she tried. His lips pressed against hers as his tongue slipped through the seam of her lips to taste the insides of her mouth. She clutched his shoulders and writhed against him, frustrated by the elusiveness of his cock as it bobbed in the water, evading her attempts to rub against him.

He kissed her long and hard, leaving her lips bruised and pleasantly tingling. She felt marked by Cliff by the time he moved his head downward, sucking forcefully on her neck. She was sure to have a hickey, and she reveled in the idea of him leaving marks on her.

His mouth moved lower still, pausing near her breasts. "What perfect tits you have. You rarely see this perfect shape and pertness unless the girl's had implants. You haven't had implants though." He spoke with confidence, indicating he wasn't asking for confirmation. He knew.

Nevertheless, she shook her head. "Of course not."

"Natural tits and a waxed pussy." His fingers drifted lightly across her mound before going to her hip. "You're the perfect package, and I can see why Michael and Daniel are both desperate to have you."

She twined her fingers through his hair, noticing a few strands of silver at the temples. That made him even sexier. "Isn't it all too soon?" She realized she was deferring to him for guidance. It seemed counterintuitive to ask if she was doing the right thing when she was sitting on his lap with her nipple almost in his mouth, but she was certain she could trust him to direct her honestly.

"It doesn't feel like it. The Warren men often know what we want, and we go after it with zeal. When I met Gayle in college, I knew she was the one for me. I had her in my bed within forty-eight hours, and my ring was on her finger in less than a week. We conceived the twins somewhere around our honeymoon, and it was because I couldn't bear not to have her stomach swelling with proof that she was mine. I would've kept her pregnant continuously in my early cavemen days, but Gayle had other plans." He chuckled ruefully. "I had to dial down some of that possessiveness over the years, and she turned me into a mostly civilized beast."

7

THE OBVIOUS LOVE AND affection in his tone didn't threaten Heather. It just made him more endearing, and she leaned down, cupping his cheeks to kiss him. When she pulled back, she asked, "She was your soulmate?"

"She was my everything. When she died ten years ago, I went through a dark period. I didn't think I could keep going. If it hadn't been for Michael and Daniel, I wouldn't have. I never expected to feel anything like that again. I thought Gayle was the only one for me. When she died, I was certain my chances of ever feeling that way about someone else were over."

He cupped her breasts, but his gaze didn't move from hers. "Until you. I can see falling hard for you, Heather. Michael already has, and Daniel's well on his way. I can't help thinking you're the missing piece of the Warren family."

She could've pointed out the strangeness of a family that shared a woman, but she didn't want to do anything to damage the moment. He was clearly pouring out his heart, and she didn't think he was being insincere or spinning her a line to convince her to fuck him.

There was no convincing needed, since her pussy was only inches away from his hard cock. His words served to seduce her, but it only added to her arousal and need for him. She didn't feel like he was manipulating her into feeling something she wouldn't have otherwise.

Once more, she kissed him with openmouthed ferocity, and his passion matched her own. She reached down between their bodies to find his cock, starting to line it up with her pussy so she could take him inside her.

With a groan, Cliff pulled away slightly. "Just a minute. There was another reason I didn't join you three today. That's because you didn't have another hole that was ready. I want to take care of that now."

She frowned in confusion. "I don't understand."

He reached behind him to the edge of the tub to grasp something, revealing a red anal plug. "I thought you could use some preparation before you try to take a cock in your ass. You are an anal virgin, aren't you?" Once again, he spoke with confidence, as though he already knew the answer.

She nodded, eyeing the plug uncertainly. "Will it hurt?"

"Maybe a little, but it feels amazing after it's inside. I promise you'll like it, especially when I stuff your sweet little pussy with my cock. You'll have so much pressure inside, you'll swear you're going to explode, but it will give you the most amazing orgasm. You can trust me."

Even though they'd only known each other a day, she was certain she could. She nodded. "What should I do?"

"Turn around and brace yourself on the edge of the tub. Stick up your hips to angle your ass upward and prop your shins on the bench."

She followed his directions, taking the position he'd indicated. A moment later, the water splashed as he sat up and moved around behind her. Cliff drizzled something warm and oily over her ass that smelled like roses, and his hands started massaging her cheeks.

She closed her eyes and enjoyed the feel of his hands gliding over her, his thumbs creeping ever closer to the forbidden pucker no one had ever breached. She'd been too afraid to try it, though she'd been intrigued by the idea. It just seemed like the reality would be too much for her, but she surrendered herself to Cliff's tutelage, gasping softly when his thumb breached her hole.

He slipped in gently, and his digit was so oiled that there was hardly any resistance. It didn't even hurt. It just felt strange, but not unpleasant. Not pleasurable either though. She turned her head to look at him. "It's okay."

He grinned. "I promise it'll be much more than okay. Does that hurt at all?" When she shook her head, he started wriggling his thumb back and forth, stretching her hole. "That?"

She nodded. "Not exactly painful, but it...stings? I don't know. It's hard to describe."

There was another squirt of oil, and it seeped around his thumb and into her anus, easing his passage. "Does it hurt now?"

She shook her head. "No." She tried not to stiffen as his other thumb breached the ring, slowly sliding inside while he parted her cheeks with his palms. She definitely felt something then. There was a twinge of discomfort, but she couldn't deny it sent a pulse of pleasure through her pussy. "That's...interesting."

Cliff chuckled. "Yes." He started thrusting his thumbs lightly in and out of her, pushing in as deeply as he could and gently pulling them apart. It started out as something to endure, but she was soon wiggling her hips and needing something more. She put her hand between her thighs and started playing with her clit while he thumb-fucked her ass. "Cliff..." She wasn't certain what she wanted to say. Her voice was thick with need, and he seemed to know exactly what to do.

"I think you're ready for the plug." His thumbs left her ass, and she was bereft at the lack of attention. How had she gone from anal virgin to craving something inside her back passage in a few scant minutes?

"Press back gently and bear down." As he spoke, he pressed the tip of the silicone plug through her pucker. She tried to breathe and relax, wincing when the wide point breached her passage a few seconds later. "I..." She was about to tell him she couldn't take it, but then the wide part was through, and the plug was all the way inside her. She could feel the rectangular base lightly pressing against her crease. She also felt overly full, but it wasn't uncomfortable. It just made her want more attention for her pussy.

"That is a beautiful sight, with your ass clenched around it. I can't wait to have my cock in there, but not right now. I'm going to give you a chance to adjust, all right?"

She nodded, incapable of speech.

"Okay, princess, I'm going to sit down on the bench again, and I want you to sit on my lap. This time, if you're ready, I'm going to put my cock inside your hot little cunt. Is that okay?"

She nodded dutifully, shocked at how his filthy words turned her on. If someone had called her a cunt, she would've been enraged, but when he said it like that, it sounded like a term of endearment. He clearly wanted her cunt with every fiber of his being, and that certainly added to her arousal as well.

Cliff sat down, helping her move to straddle him. It was strange to feel the toy in her backside, but it didn't seem to be in danger of dislodging. Then he reached between their bodies, two of his fingers surging inside her sheath. She whimpered at the sensation, which hovered on the edge of overstuffed and too much. She wondered how much more intense it would be when his cock entered her, and she didn't have to wait long to find out.

8

AFTER FINDING THE PATH, he guided himself into her, at first thrusting shallowly in and out of her pussy, letting her get accommodated to his girth. He was certainly larger than his sons. She was afraid he'd be too much for her, but slowly, he rocked his way inside her until she was finally settled snugly on his lap.

She clung to him, thighs tightening around his legs, as he tilted her angle slightly so he could be completely inside her. She could practically taste him at the back of her throat, she thought with a little giggle.

He arched a brow. "What's so funny, princess?"

"Just imagining your cock is so big and deep inside me that it's practically in my throat."

He let out a growl of pleasure. "I wouldn't mind having my cock in your throat later, but it feels too amazing in your cunt right now. How do you feel? Are you squeezed and overstuffed with me inside you, and the toy in your ass?"

She nodded, not holding back. "It's so much. I don't know if I can do this."

He started strumming her clit. "I have every faith in your ability to do this. Besides, think of the greater good."

She frowned. "I don't understand."

"If you want to be able to take all three Warren men at the same time, you need to be prepared for that. You can't just jump into having your sweet asshole filled up with one cock, with another cocky in your pussy, and your mouth wrapped around a third. Preparing for that is for the greater good." He winked.

The imagery his words evoked sent a renewed surge of arousal through her, and it helped overcome the last of her discomfort as he started to move inside her. With each thrust, she lost the lingering hesitation from some of the overwhelming sensations filling her, and she was soon enjoying being stuffed that way.

She imagined the toy was one of the twins with his cock in her ass, while she stared into Cliff's eyes and rode him. He held her hips, controlling the thrust and the pace as he lifted her up his cock and slid her down again while she twisted her hips in a circular motion, dragging out the sensation of his cockhead pulsing against her g-spot, feeling herself on the verge of coming.

"Play with your tits. I want to see you roll those pretty little nipples between your fingers."

She tossed back her head and brought up her hands to comply with his commands, tugging and stroking her nipples forcefully. It was much rougher than she normally touched herself, but she was caught up in the moment, and it was perfect.

"I'm going to come soon. Are you on the edge of coming with me? I don't want to go without you, princess."

"Almost...?" Her body was such a mass of sensations that she couldn't be sure what was happening or when it would happen. She was just consumed with pleasure.

"Almost isn't good enough." He renewed stroking her clit, rubbing his thumb firmly underneath the hood until she was sobbing and arching against him wildly despite his hand on one of her hips still trying to rein her in. She couldn't be contained though.

She fucked him with wild abandon until her orgasm crested, and she splintered apart in his arms. Cliff let out a husky growl, his face buried against her chest, as his cum spurted inside her. He held her tightly against him, hands returning to both her hips, as he twitched and convulsed until every drop of his seed had finished pulsing into her. Even then, he didn't separate their bodies. He just held her against him for several moments as they recovered from their release.

Abruptly realizing she was still squeezing her nipples, this time hard enough to hurt, she dropped her hands from them to put around his neck. She snuggled closer as his face nestled between her breasts, his tongue flicking out to lick one of her nipples in passing.

The toy had stayed inside her, and she was bracing herself for some pain when he pulled it out a few seconds later. There was a hint of discomfort, but it wasn't bad at all. Then his hand moved to her ass, fingers wiggling inside lightly to clean her hole before he separated their bodies. She was still slick inside from his cum, and it made her horny all over again.

Cliff must've realized that, because he lifted her effortlessly from the water and placed her on the floor, legs splayed so he could get to her pussy. He didn't seem at all deterred that he had just come inside her as he started licking her with sure, deep, and firm strokes. When he sucked hard on her clit, she had another small orgasm, and she finally felt sated for the moment.

Afterward, he carried her to the shower, washing them both off as she plastered herself against him. "With three lovers, I don't think I'll ever have the energy to do anything except sex," she said with a laugh when he set her on the bathmat a few minutes later and started toweling her off.

She stood there passively, allowing him to take care of her, because he seemed to enjoy it. She enjoyed it too, and though she was incapable of mustering the enthusiasm for another round of sex, she was still pulsing between her thighs with pleasure.

It was a spontaneous act when she dropped to her knees on the bathmat to grasp the base of his cock, guiding it toward her mouth. Cliff wrapped her hair around one of his large hands and held her mouth against him while she took his cock inside, letting it nestle at the base of her throat.

This time, he really was at the back of her throat, and it was amazing. Her lips had barely been able to stretch wide enough to accommodate him, and she marveled again that he'd managed to fit that monster in her pussy while she had the toy in her ass. She hoped that meant she'd be able to take all three Warren men the next time they were ready to play.

She moved her mouth almost lazily, gently massaging him with her cheeks and her tongue. He was hard and thick, and he started thrusting against her face. When his cock went deeper in her throat than any man's had been, she choked for a moment, and he stilled.

He didn't withdraw though. "Breathe through it, princess. I know you can do it."

Determined to please him, she took a deep breath, which also seemed to arouse him further, and relaxed as much as she could. The feeling of choking passed, and she was soon sucking wildly.

When he rewarded her by coming, she swallowed every drop before sitting on her calves and staring up at him. It was a subservient position, but it felt right. There was definitely something dominant about Cliff.

She wondered if Michael and Daniel would inherit it as well, eventually growing into similar demanding, confident men. The idea of being at the mercy of three dominant Warrens made her pussy wet again, but she was too tired and sore to imagine taking another cock just then.

Cliff lifted her to her feet, carrying her to his bed and putting her in it. He joined her, curling up with his hand on her stomach, and his semi-flaccid cock resting between the cheeks of her ass. One of his hands moved to her breast, cupping it possessively. He tweaked the nipple every few minutes, but mostly allowed her to rev down.

Soon, sleep overtook her, and she cuddled against her boyfriend's father, acknowledging he was now her boyfriend as well. Boyfriend seemed too tame of a word though. He was her lover, just like Daniel and Michael. Her life had certainly taken a sharp turn in the last twenty-four hours, but she was optimistic it would end up being a wonderful thing. Anything that felt this good couldn't be bad.

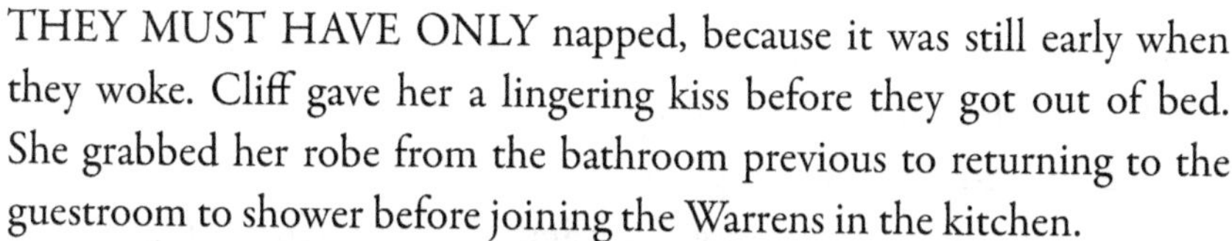

9

THEY MUST HAVE ONLY napped, because it was still early when they woke. Cliff gave her a lingering kiss before they got out of bed. She grabbed her robe from the bathroom previous to returning to the guestroom to shower before joining the Warrens in the kitchen.

The scent of pancakes greeted her as Daniel manned the griddle. Michael was making freshly squeezed orange juice, and she uttered a sound of delight. "I could get used to this," she said as she took the plate of pancakes Daniel offered her. Michael swatted her butt as she passed him to get a glass of OJ, and she squealed before rushing to the table.

A sense of camaraderie filled the atmosphere as they sat at the table around her. She supposed she should feel shy and awkward around them, but it was difficult to feel like they were strangers when she'd had each of these men inside her over the last twenty-four hours.

"What are your plans now that you've graduated?" Cliff asked Michael.

Michael shrugged. "I need to send out some resumes. I might get my real estate license. It's required if I want to get into developing and brokering."

"That's a sound choice. I didn't know you were interested in that line of work." Cliff dabbed his mouth, wiping at a stubborn patch of maple syrup that Heather wanted to volunteer to lick away for him. "You should have told me when I sold the company a few years ago."

"What company?" asked Heather.

Cliff looked at her. "I owned a commercial real estate development firm, but I sold it when I got a good offer a few years back. It was time." He looked sad for a moment. "Gayle helped me build it up to what it became. If I'd known Michael wanted to take a crack at it, I'd have kept it in trust for him, or at least negotiated a position with him with the new owners."

Michael waved a hand. "I knew you were ready to be done with it, Dad, and I want to do this on my own—though I wouldn't mind some advice from you."

"Gladly," said Cliff as he turned his attention to Daniel. "What about you, son? Did you get that interview with the music school?"

Heather looked at him. "Music school? You're a musician?"

He nodded. "Guitar and piano."

"That explains the callouses." Seeing his perplexed expression, she said, "Your fingers are more calloused than Michael's."

He nodded his comprehension. "Yeah. And to answer your question, Dad, no, I didn't. They want someone with more experience, so I'll probably give lessons for a while."

Cliff nodded, not pushing him to do anything more. Perhaps Heather shouldn't have been surprised, since he'd sold his own company well before retirement age, but she'd expected their father to put more pressure on both of them.

Speaking of pressure, he turned to look at her next. "What do you plan to do with your bachelor's degree, Heather?"

She swallowed the orange juice in her mouth. "Um, I guess send out resumes. I interviewed for some spots before graduation, and I did well at an internship, but they didn't hire me. It's hard to find a job right now."

He nodded. "You should take your time. You're welcome to stay with us as long as you'd like...no strings."

She flushed and looked down but nodded as she did so. She appreciated him making it clear she wasn't there just for sex. Not that she minded the sex, though she was still sore from all of yesterday and this morning's activities.

"Do you have plans today?" asked Cliff, his gaze touching on all three of them. When they shook their heads, he smiled. "Let's take out the yacht."

Her eyes widened. They had a yacht? Of course they did. Living in this neighborhood, it was probably required to have a yacht at the marina, like having a car in the garage. When he asked if she liked sailing, she shrugged. "I don't know. I've only been on a couple of harbor cruises. I liked those just fine."

"No seasickness?"

"Nope."

Cliff looked satisfied. "Excellent. Everyone, grab your gear, and we'll head out in twenty minutes." He wiped his mouth and stood up, taking his plate and glass to the sink. The twins followed a second later, and Heather finished her last bite and gulped the rest of the juice to keep up.

HARBOR CRUISES HAD little in common with sailing. There were waves and the rocking motion, but the harbor boats she'd been on had been utilitarian. This was pure luxury, including multiple staterooms. Partway through the day, having easily gained her sea legs, she stood by Cliff as he showed her how to steer the boat. She grinned at him. "I could live out here."

His eyes sparkled for a moment, but his expression reverted to one that was less mysterious a second later. "I concur."

"Was this yours and Gayle's boat?" she asked.

Cliff moved to stand behind her, putting his arms around her waist. "No. Gayle hated the water. She never learned to swim and had horrible seasickness. I bought the yacht after I sold the business and spent a year sailing around the world while the boys were in their freshman year of college."

She leaned against him with a dreamy sigh. "Oh, that sounds wonderful."

"You'd like that?"

She nodded eagerly before it turned to a moan when he thumbed her nipple through her thin top. She hadn't bothered with a bra, but she'd brought her swimsuit. Maybe she should have worn it under her top instead of stuffing it in her bag. The nipple pebbled at his expert plucking, and she writhed against him.

"I'm going to drop anchor for a bit, guys," called Cliff as he stepped back from her. "Let's sunbathe. No one's around."

She moved to Michael and Daniel, who'd laid two large blankets across the deck despite the deck chairs. She suspected it was so they could all lie down together. Her stomach fluttered as she wondered if they all planned to fuck her now. She was a little nervous but mostly excited.

Heather went to her bag to retrieve her bikini, but Daniel came up behind her and took it out of her hand. "We don't need those."

She turned when she felt his cock brush her hip, finding him naked. Michael was shedding his shorts as well, and Cliff walked toward them with his cock hard and jutting forward. Her mouth was dry, but she nodded and let go of the bikini. When Daniel helped pull up her tank top, she lifted her arms to let him.

She put her fingers in the waistband of her shorts, hooking her panties as well, and pushed them down with a deep breath for courage. When she stood up, Daniel put his arm around her back to guide her to the sunning spot. Michael was already lying down on the deck, while Cliff perched on a lounger.

Acting on instinct, Heather crawled to Michael, enjoying the indrawn breaths from Daniel and Cliff, who had a close view of her pussy from that position. She knelt over Michael before leaning down to give him a long kiss. He held her face in his hands and kept her mouth against his for a long moment, not letting go until she grasped his cock. "Are you going to suck me?"

She shrugged. "Unless you want something else?"

Her boyfriend grinned. "A blowjob is good...for now."

10

SHE BENT HER HEAD, her ass still in the air, and licked him from base to tip before swirling her tongue around the corona. He stiffened and arched against her, urging her to take his length. She did so, pushing past the previous limit she'd known with Michael to let him settle deep in her throat.

"Oh, fuck," he whispered harshly, eyes closed as the cords in his neck strained.

"Fuck yeah," said Daniel as he knelt behind Heather.

She froze for a second as he parted her thighs and her cheeks, expecting him to engage in ass play. Instead, he was just parting the way to bury his mouth against her slit and start licking her like a starving man.

She sucked Michael as he bucked against her face, loving the glimpses of his expression she could see. It was intoxicating to give him such pleasure. She was frankly amazed she could continue to do so with Daniel's tongue moving so expertly through her pussy, bring her to the verge of coming.

"I'm going to burst," said Michael, grasping a handful of her long blonde hair. "Do you want to swallow?"

She nodded her enthusiasm. Her answer was always yes, but he still often asked her. She found it considerate and caring that he did so. His shaft twitched a moment later, and he came in her throat. She swallowed the cum before he eased back.

Daniel pushed her down with her face firmly against the deck. The position was humbling, leaving her vulnerable and at his mercy—a place that didn't frighten her. He kept licking her until she grasped the blanket under her and cried out during her orgasm.

She'd barely recovered from that when strong hands lifted her into a pair of equally strong arms. She smiled at Cliff as she weathered the aftermath of her orgasm. He carried her to the lounger he'd been on, propping her on his lap with her back to his stomach. She glimpsed a tube of something she initially identified as sunscreen until he brought it closer, and she was able to read the word "lube" on the tube. She trembled slightly.

"Do you want to stop?" asked Cliff when she shuddered against him. "You don't have to do anything you don't want to do."

She nodded. "I know. I want to do this. I'm just a little nervous."

He put his palm over her abdomen. "Remember how good it felt this morning with that toy in your ass and my cock in your pussy?" At her nod, he dipped his hand lower to brush against her waxed mound. "It'll be just as good this time. Maybe even better. Okay, princess?"

She nodded her agreement and leaned forward when Cliff guided her to do so. The tip of the lube pressed against her pucker a moment later, and then cool, slippery lubricant filled her back passage. She maintained that pose until he guided her back to sitting on his lap again.

He addressed his sons when he spoke next. "I'm going to get in her ass and make sure she's comfortable before you join in. We don't want to hurt her."

"Never," said Michael fervently.

"Wouldn't dream of it," said Daniel.

She gave them both bright smiles as Cliff guided the tip of his cock, which seemed impossibly wide at the moment, to her pucker. Remembering how he'd had her bear down before, she did that instinctively as he pressed against the stubborn ring of muscle. Moving slowly, he slipped inside with a pop seconds later, holding back and feeding an inch at a time deeper inside her.

She gasped at the intrusion and the stinging sensation, but it faded by the time he was fully inside her. Then he wrapped his arms around her and leaned back on the lounge, pulling her atop him with her back against his chest. He grasped her hips and adjusted their positions slightly.

"How is it?" asked Michael, his eyes full of concern.

Heather smiled. "It's okay."

"Fucking heaven," said Cliff. "Your ass is like a vice, princess. You're squeezing my dick so hard."

"Is that a good thing?" she asked with a hint of uncertainty.

"Very," said Cliff with a grunt. "I think she's ready for you boys now."

She tried to relax and open her legs as wide as possible when Michael reached her. He'd gotten hard again already, and his cock nudged her slick entrance. His eyes widened when he tried to slide inside her. She frowned. "Is something wrong?"

He shook his head. "You're just so damned tight." He closed his eyes and worked his cock inside. Once the head was past the entrance, he slid in the rest of the way with ease. Michael tossed back his head and shouted something unintelligible before saying, "So good."

It was good for her too, though it was also painful. It wasn't like this morning. She was far fuller with their two large cocks inside her. She didn't tell them it was uncomfortable, choosing to breathe through it instead. She wanted this to work. She was determined to make it happen.

Michael shifted slightly, and suddenly, things changed. She was still overstuffed with cock, but it wasn't painful. It just felt like too much, but in a good way.

Daniel must have been waiting for that moment, because he approached now, standing to the side of her as he lazily stroked his cock. She turned her head to wrap her lips around the head, and he thrust forward to push his thick shaft fully inside her. He hit the back of her throat and kept going. She had to breathe around his cock, and she was still focusing on breathing through the intense sensations of having Cliff and Michael both fucking her. The Warren men left her breathless.

Daniel started thrusting in and out of her mouth, doing most of the work. He must have realized she wasn't as focused as she needed to be right then to give a good blowjob. She maintained suction and kept her cheeks wrapped around him though.

Cliff and Michael had found a rhythm, and they were also doing all the work. She couldn't move between them. They moved her as their cocks slipped in and out of her in opposing meter. It was the perfect way to handle the position, since it kept her from feeling overly stuffed but still allowed her to feel every inch of their cocks thrusting in and out of her.

The first orgasm sneaked up on her, and she surrendered to it with a squeal of surprise. It was hard to keep track of everything happening to her body, so she just surrendered and went with it as Michael and Cliff brought her to the edge of another release moments later. Daniel's cock tightened her in her mouth, but he pulled out before he could cum.

She gasped when his warm arousal splashed her breasts a moment later, and she lifted her hands to rub in his cum, remembering how Cliff had done the same yesterday when he came on her chest. It felt good, and she enjoyed having Daniel's seed on her skin.

"Fuck," said Cliff softly, his cock stiffening.

Michael's was twitching inside her as he spilled his seed. She wondered if Cliff had cursed because the convulsions transmitted through her sheath had pushed him to the edge as they vibrated through to her ass. His hands grasped hard to her hips as he pulled her back against him. Michael was slowly pulling out, and Cliff climaxed a second later with a harsh grunt and copious amounts of release filling her back passage.

She collapsed against Cliff's chest as they both took time to gather their breath. A few minutes later, Michael picked her up and laid her on the blanket beside him. Daniel laid on her other side, and Cliff stretched out near her feet. He took one in his hand and started massaging it gently.

The wind was blowing, but it was pleasant, even on her naked body. The waves, combined with the exhaustion following that amazing sex, were lulling her to sleep. She stirred only when Cliff tickled her foot, recoiling and moaning in protest.

"How do you like sailing, princess?"

She lifted her head to meet his gaze. "I love it, especially with the Warren men." She could definitely get used to this.

11

THE WEEKS HAD STARTED to blend together in a haze of lovemaking and relaxation. Heather had yet to send out another round of resumes, and she knew Michael was slacking just as much. She kept putting it off until tomorrow, because today brought such lovely treats every day.

It was physically demanding to satisfy three lovers, but the tradeoff was she'd never been so sated in her life. And they spoiled her rotten, pampering her smallest whim. She didn't want to take it for granted or expect such treatment, so she made sure to be appreciative of each thing they did for her, big or small.

Her mind was on them when she answered her phone, so she didn't bother to look at the caller ID. "Hello?"

"Hi, kiddo, it's your mom." Cheryl sounded close to tears.

She grimaced, knowing this would be another session where Cheryl complained about her latest lover dumping her. "I recognize your voice." She didn't sound warm when she answered.

If Cheryl noticed, she ignored the lack of warmth. "Paul and I are taking a break. I thought we could spend some time together?"

"I don't have my own place, and neither do you. I don't think that would work." She clung to the excuse, looking up as Michael entered the living room where she'd sprawled on the huge sectional.

"You must be staying somewhere."

"With my boyfriend," she said grudgingly. "Do you remember Michael? You met him a few months ago when you stopped by in January to deliver my Christmas present and stayed thirty minutes." Bitterness bled through her tone and Michael responded by coming to sit beside her and lean against her.

"Sure, I remember him. Nice young man. Surely, he doesn't mind if I stay with you for a few days?"

She felt trapped as she looked at Michael. "She's asking to visit. Please say no," she whispered.

Michael must not have heard the last part, because he shrugged. "I'm sure Dad won't care. There's an extra guestroom, or you can move into my room for the visit and let her use your room."

Heather had kept the guestroom for the past few weeks, since it gave her freedom to choose with whom she wanted to spend each night. She alternated between the three of them regularly, and more than once, they'd fallen asleep on this very sectional after a long round of vigorous sex involving all three of her lovers and her.

"Excellent," said Cheryl loudly enough for Heather to wince even though her mother wasn't on speakerphone. "Text me the address." After Heather did so, she said, "I'm in the area, so I'll be there this afternoon."

"I can't wait," said Heather with a touch of sourness before hanging up. She turned to Michael. "I told you to say no."

He put up a hand. "I'm not going to be the bad guy. I want your mom to like me."

"What's going on?" asked Cliff as he entered the living room. Daniel appeared moments later with his guitar case, clearly on his way to teach a private lesson.

"Cheryl, Heather's mom, invited herself to stay with us for a few days. I hope that's okay?" asked Michael.

Cliff frowned. "Sure, I guess. Does your mother know about our arrangement, Heather?" When she shook her head, he frowned. "I don't like secrets."

She licked her lips. "I don't either. I don't want to hide anything."

"But maybe we should ease into telling her," said Daniel. "It could be a shock."

Heather frowned. "I don't really care if it is."

Michael sighed. "I know she's hurt you a lot, but do you really want to reveal you have three boyfriends abruptly?"

She shrugged and then stilled. "Are you all my boyfriends?"

"Sure," said Michael, looking confused.

"I thought so," said Daniel.

She looked at Cliff, who grimaced. "Boyfriend is such a tepid word, but yeah."

She looked down at her clasped hands for a moment. "We haven't discussed where this is going, you know?"

"I've been living in the moment," said Daniel carelessly. "I expect to have lots of moments with you in our future."

She let out a shaky breath at his encouraging words. "So you want a future?"

Daniel put down the case and came to stand behind her. He put his hands on her shoulders and leaned down so their faces were close together, if upside down. "I can't picture a future without you."

Her lips wobbled for a moment, and she smiled at him before turning her head when Michael nudged her chin.

"I have a ring upstairs. I've had it since three weeks after we started dating. I didn't want to rush the proposal, but I've been planning to ask. Part of the reason I held off was I suspected Daniel would want you as much as I do." He looked at his dad with a grin of amusement. "Dad was a bit of a surprise, but it feels perfect. I'm ready to propose if you want me to, but I'm fine with you not marrying any of us if that's how you want to do it. I'm definitely all-in and want to be with you."

She blinked back tears before glancing at Cliff, who'd been mostly mute. She was questioning with her eyes, but he was evading her gaze. Finally, she asked, "Cliff, how do you feel?"

He sighed heavily. "I definitely feel a connection with you. I didn't expect to have that again. Part of me is ready to go for it, just like I did with Gayle, but I'm also afraid to truly commit again. I barely survived losing her. I can't go through that again."

She looked down. "Oh." It was a sensible and honest reply, but it felt like he'd ripped out her heart and stomped on it. "What does that mean for us?" She looked up again.

"I want to be with you, but I'm not ready for this discussion. I just need a little more time, if you can spare it?" Cliff smiled at her when she nodded. "I care a lot. I just need to sort it out, princess."

She nodded and soon allowed Michael to distract her with a trip to the store to ensure they had her mother's favorites on hand. Daniel had gone off to his lesson, and Cliff was headed for his study when they left. She was only a few miles from him, but it felt like thousands at the moment.

CHERYL ARRIVED THAT afternoon, blowing in like a hurricane, with roughly the same destructive force on Heather's peace of mind. She greeted the older woman with a hug and led her to the living room after introducing her to Daniel and reminding her who Michael was. Cliff was out for a jog, so he got to delay the meeting. Lucky guy.

"This is some place you have," said Cheryl as she tossed back a shot of vodka she'd asked for within moments of arriving.

"It's not my place." But it felt like home. If Cliff decided he couldn't commit to her, she and Michael would find another place, and she was sure Daniel would join them. She wouldn't be alone, but she wouldn't be complete either.

"Play your cards right, and it can be. Get the ring on your finger as soon as you can. Don't wait until you're in your forties and desperate." Cheryl poured another shot and downed it like water.

Heather avoided addressing that uncomfortable piece of advice. "How long are you staying?"

"Just until I regroup. I figured a couple of days, but maybe a couple of weeks, since this place is so swanky, and there's room to spread out."

She glared at her mother. "You aren't imposing on Cliff's hospitality for two weeks, Mom."

Cheryl tipped her head. "Where is Cliff? He's the father of the twins—and lord, what handsome boys they are—right? How do you tell them apart?" She laughed. "I guess that's easy. Only one is your boyfriend."

"Er, right. Cliff's out for a run." Heather's stomach knotted as she analyzed her mom's obvious interest. "You aren't—" Before she could warn her mother off trying to go after Cliff, he appeared in the entryway, still in his jogging clothes with sweat stains that looked sexy on him. She closed her eyes briefly when Cheryl shifted on the couch, angling her body closer to the doorway, so Cliff could see down her blouse.

"You must be Cliff." Cheryl virtually purred the words as she stood up and sashayed toward him. "I can see where your sons get their handsomeness from."

Cliff darted a look at Heather before looking back at Cheryl when she placed her hand on his chest. He lifted it off and turned it into a handshake before stepping back. "And you must be Cheryl. It's nice to meet you. If you'll excuse me, I need to take a shower."

"Want help washing your back?" asked Cheryl with a coy giggle.

Cliff didn't answer, but he did run up the stairs, as though fleeing a pack of wild dogs. He must have realized Cheryl had claws instead of teeth, and she wanted to dig them into his flesh.

Heather was annoyed with her mother's behavior, but she wasn't certain how to call her on it without warning her away from Cliff because he was Heather's lover. She doubted Cheryl was ready to hear that.

"He's a sexy beast. I wonder what he's like in the sack." Cheryl returned to her seat to pour a third shot of vodka.

Dominant and possessive, but with a tender streak a mile wide. She didn't say that aloud. "Don't even think about it."

Cheryl frowned. "It would be so perfect. You're with Mitchell—"

"Michael," she corrected in irritation.

Her mother waved a hand. "Cliff is single, right?" At Heather's grudging nod, she grinned. "See, perfect. We could be one big, happy family."

Heather shuddered at the idea. "No."

Cheryl rolled her eyes. "Don't ruin this for me, baby. I need a security blanket. I'm getting older and losing my looks." She whispered the last part. "I need a man to take care of me."

"Or you could take care of yourself," snapped Heather. "Use your degree in library sciences."

Her mother looked sullen. "I can't. Hardly anyone hires librarians with only a bachelor's these days, and my degree is twenty-three years old. I'm not qualified for any jobs."

She counted to ten to maintain her patience. "You can go back to school, or you can look outside your field. You don't need a man to watch over you."

Cheryl let out a sob. "It's different for me. I'm a different kind of woman. Snagging a man like Cliff would solve all my problems."

"Until you created more," muttered Heather. With a tired sigh, she stood up. "Let me show you the guestroom." She led her mother up to the room across the hall from hers and left her there. She couldn't take anymore at the moment.

12

CHERYL DIDN'T BACK off. She doubled down, coming down for dinner in a dress that was slit up to her hip and displayed most of her bosom. Heather was embarrassed at the sight and hid her head against Daniel's shoulder, since he was the closest one. That was the first of many cringeworthy moments as her mother made it clear to Cliff that he could have her if he wanted her.

He looked trapped and managed to evade her advances for the evening. Before dessert, he excused himself to make a business call. Heather was skeptical, since he didn't have much business to attend to these days, aside from some rental homes he maintained, and the time he spent on wealth management. She couldn't blame him for fleeing.

Her mother had been liberal with the alcohol too. She followed Heather and the twins into the living room. When they sat on either side of Heather, Cheryl made a purring sound. "How devilishly tempting. However do you keep your hands off Damian?" She was eyeing Daniel like a piece of meat, and he shifted with a scared look. He was like a bunny who'd just scented a cougar. If anyone met the definition, it was her mother.

Driven to the point of not being able to take more of her mother's crap that evening, Heather put her hand on the thigh of each man. "I don't. I'm dating Mitchell and Damian," she said with heavy sarcasm, figuring her mother wouldn't remember this in the morning with the way she was imbibing.

Cheryl faltered for a moment, the cougar slipping to reveal the briefest flash of a concerned mother. "Really? Is that wise, baby? I don't want you to get hurt."

"We aren't going to hurt her," said Michael firmly.

"We love her," added Daniel as he put his arm around her shoulders.

With a blink, Cheryl shrugged. "If it works for you, who am I to judge? You'll have double the security if you can hang onto them, Heather."

Heather rolled her eyes. "It's late. I'm going to bed." She gave a pointed look to Michael and Daniel, who followed her out of the room. Cheryl was moving toward the liquor cabinet. Maybe she should intercede, but she was the daughter, not the mother, and it wasn't her place to keep Cheryl from making bad decisions.

LATER THAT NIGHT, AFTER Daniel and Michael found blissful ways to distract her from her problems, she slipped out of Michael's room, leaving the twins both snoring in the king-size bed, to check on her mother. Guilt was getting to her, and she wanted to ensure Cheryl hadn't passed out in the living room with the bottle of vodka at her side.

She heard voices as she neared the living room, and when she stepped inside, her mouth dropped open in outrage. Her mother had backed Cliff into a corner and was pressing her body against him. His hands weren't engaging, other than to stop hers from getting overly familiar. He was clearly trapped, wanting to be kind without being violated. When his eyes met hers, his relief was palpable.

She rushed forward. "Enough of this, Mom. Get away from Cliff right now."

Cheryl was clearly tipsy—or outright drunk—because she stumbled a bit when she turned to Heather. "I told you not to mess this up for me, Heather."

"He doesn't want you," she said in exasperation.

"How do you know?" Cheryl hiccupped. "I know all kinds of ways to interest a man."

"Not this one, you don't. Get your hands off my lover right now."

Cheryl stiffened, as did Cliff. When she reeled back, it allowed him to make his escape, and he came to stand behind Heather, putting a hand on her hip and his arm around her waist.

"What are you...? He's old enough to be your father, and you have those twins." Cheryl's eyes were red. "You can't have all three. Give me one of them, you selfish brat."

Heather flinched. "You're going to sober up at some point and regret what you're doing. Let's stop before we say unforgivable things."

"No. It's your fault I'm alone. I turned down a man who wanted to marry me when you were in high school because he didn't want you. He wouldn't wait until you went to college. You can't rob me of a future and then do it again with him." She stabbed her finger in Cliff's direction.

Heather's lip curled. "For goodness sake, Dad died in April the year I graduated high school. Someone proposed to you within weeks of his death?"

Cheryl shrugged. "He'd always liked me, but you ruined it. Not this time."

"Enough," said Cliff firmly. "You will be leaving my house right away, Mrs. Ross. Until you learn some respect, you aren't welcome back."

Cheryl glared at him. "She owes me—"

Cliff turned away from her, leaving the room. Heather felt abandoned, but she couldn't blame him for jumping ship before it went down in flames. "You can't drive like this, so I'll call you a cab."

"I have nowhere to go and no money to go with. This is all your fault. You always were a wicked child. And slutting with three men?" Cheryl staggered closer. "I'm disgusted by you."

"The feeling is mutual." Heather stiffened when Cliff reappeared, eyes widening as he held out a check to her mother. "Don't give her any money."

"She's still your mother, and without her, you wouldn't be in my life." He turned to Cheryl. "There's a cab on the way, and I took the liberty of gathering your bag from the guestroom while I was upstairs writing the check. You can wait outside for the cab. Don't contact Heather again unless you're prepared to be a real mother to her—and don't come back for more handouts. This is a one-time deal."

Heather's eyes widened when she saw the number of zeroes. "That's a crazy amount."

"Money well spent," said Cliff as he took her mother by the arm and led her to the front door. He opened it, undeterred by Cheryl's pleas, and pushed her through firmly. He set her bag on the stoop and closed the door before engaging the lock.

Heather couldn't believe he'd given her mother a check. "She didn't do anything to deserve that."

He shrugged. "I can't let your mother be without resources, but I meant that it's the only time she'll get help from us unless she cleans up and makes some changes. We aren't going to have her darting in and out of our lives for the next fifty years, stirring up drama."

Her mouth opened. "Fifty years? Does that mean you want to be with me?"

Cliff looked sheepish. "Of course. I panicked at the reality earlier, but I'd already decided on my jog that I was a fool. I'd planned to tell you I'm completely invested in a future with you and the twins, but your mother was here, and she's scary."

She laughed as she moved closer to kiss him, hearing footsteps on the stairs. "She can be, but you handled her."

"I was afraid I couldn't. She had eight hands, at least."

She laughed harder. "Maybe, but you extricated yourself, and you love me."

He nodded, his expression sincere as he gazed into her eyes. "I never expected to love again, but I've been privileged to have two special women grace my life. I do love you." He tipped her chin up for a long kiss as headlights arced through the window.

Michael and Daniel joined them then, and Cliff gave a recap as Heather walked to the window and looked out. She observed her mother get in the cab and watched until it disappeared. She doubted she'd ever see her mother again, though she clung to a small hope.

Turning away from the window, she decided it didn't matter. She had her own family right in front of her, and the Warrens were all she needed.

Epilogue

Several months later

WHEN CLIFF SUGGESTED they spend some time traveling around on the yacht, Heather had been more than willing to put her career prospects, few as they'd been, on hiatus for a while. Michael was quickly on board, and Daniel had agreed once he found someone to cover his lessons. They'd spent the last several months sailing from one exotic locale to another, and she'd fallen ever deeper in love with Michael, Daniel, and Cliff.

That had brought them to the Kinnaur region of India, which was one of the few places where a woman could legally marry more than one husband. They'd had a traditional ceremony, and the village hosting it had gone all out. It was an authentic experience, down to her decorative sari and henna.

And when it was over, and they'd gone to their lodgings for the night, Heather lost herself in the arms of her husbands. As she pleasured and was pleased by each of them, she couldn't imagine being happier or more blessed, except with a child.

That was the next project she and the Warren men were going to tackle, and she knew they'd be up for the job. By this time next year, she'd have a miniature version of her husbands, if fortune smiled on them. In the meantime, she intended to keep loving her men with all her heart and living each day with them fully. She'd never regret falling for the Warrens.

About Kit Kyndall

Kit Kyndall is the pen name *USA Today* bestselling author Kit Tunstall uses when writing contemporary erotic romances. It's simply a way to separate the myriad types of stories she writes so readers know what to expect with each "author."

Join Kit's Mailing List[1] **to keep up with new releases and receive exclusive content.**

---

1. http://eepurl.com/bpdvb9

Did you love *Falling For The Warrens*? Then you should read *Double Delights*[2] by Kit Kyndall!

What's worse than losing your fiancé? Having him break the news two weeks before the wedding during dinner with his family. Tamsyn is shamed by the way Will handles things, but so grateful when his identical brothers step in to take care of her.

It turns out Dean and Evan want to do more than care for the curvy beauty. The men share everything, and Tamsyn is just the wife they want. If she's brave enough to explore the option, she might find they are exactly what she needs.

---

2. https://books2read.com/u/3yP1zV

3. https://books2read.com/u/3yP1zV

Also by Kit Kyndall

Kingwood Prep
Catching His Eye

Protectors
Safe Harbor
Hart & Soal

Pure Escapes
Ablaze
Out Of Bounds
Guarded
Succumb
Taking
Proposition
I'm No Saint Nick

Sage Valley
Reunion

A Second Chance

Seen
Catching His Eye, Part 1
Catching His Eye, Pt. 2
Catching His Eye, Pt. 3

SpicyShorts
Pawn
Two Cowboys for Cady
Ebony Enigma
Wrong Groom
Model Behavior
Biology Lessons
Mai Tais on the Beach
All Grown Up
SpicyShorts Bundle

Sweet Escapes
Falling For A Firefighter
Worth Waiting

Well...
Well-Seasoned

Standalone
Playing His Game
Snowbound
Student Bodies
Double Delights
Tied To You
Seduction
A Royal Pain
The Island
Submission
Falling For The Warrens
Billionaire's Baby Contract

www.ingramcontent.com/pod-product-compliance
Lightning Source LLC
Chambersburg PA
CBHW061336120726
48001CB00002B/887